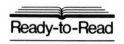
Ready-to-Read

Mitchell Is Moving

By Marjorie Weinman Sharmat

Pictures by
Jose Aruego & Ariane Dewey

MACMILLAN PUBLISHING CO., INC.
New York
COLLIER MACMILLAN PUBLISHERS
London

Macmillan Publishing Co., Inc., 866 Third Avenue, New York, N.Y. 10022
Collier Macmillan Canada, Ltd.
Printed in the United States of America

10 9 8 7 6 5 4 3 2 1

LIBRARY OF CONGRESS CATALOGING IN PUBLICATION DATA
Sharmat, Marjorie Weinman. Mitchell is moving. (Ready-to-Read)
SUMMARY: A dinosaur's exuberance about moving cools considerably
when he realizes how much he misses his next-door friend.
[1. Moving, Household—Fiction.   2. Friendship—Fiction.   3. Dinosaurs—Fiction]
I. Aruego, Jose.   II. Dewey, Ariane.   III. Title.
PZ7.S5299Mi   [E]   78-6816   ISBN 0-02-782410-1

For Mitchell
and our good move of February 24th
with love

Mitchell ran through his house.
"So long. So long, everything,"
he shouted.

Then he ran next door
to Margo's house.
"I'm moving," he said.
"Where?" asked Margo.
"Two weeks away," said Mitchell.
"Where is that?" asked Margo.

"It's wherever I will be
after I walk for two weeks,"
said Mitchell. "I have lived
in the same place
for a long time.
It is time for me
to go someplace else."

"No!" said Margo. "You have only
lived next door
for fifty years."
"Sixty," said Mitchell.
"Fifty, sixty. What's the difference?"
said Margo. "I want you to stay
next door forever."

"I can't," said Mitchell.
"I do not want to wake up
in the same old bedroom
and eat breakfast
in the same old kitchen
and brush my scales
and clean my nails
in the same old bathroom.
Every room in my house
is the same old room
because I have been there
too long."

"Well, maybe you are just tired
of the same old friend," said Margo.
"Who is that?" asked Mitchell.
"Me," said Margo.
"Maybe you look at me
and think,
'Same Old Face.
Same Old Tail.
Same Old Scales.
Same Old Walk.
Same Old Talk.
Same Old Margo.'"

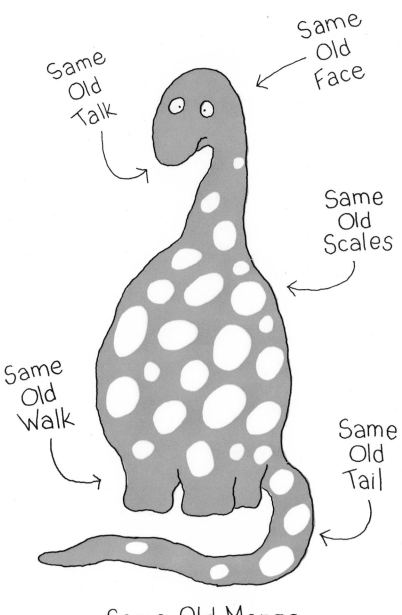

Same Old Talk

Same Old Face

Same Old Scales

Same Old Walk

Same Old Tail

Same Old Margo

"No," said Mitchell.
"I like your face, tail,
    scales, walk and talk.
    I like you."
"I like, like, like you,"
    said Margo.
"I like, like, like you, too,"
    said Mitchell.

He walked to the door.

"I must pack," he said.

Margo sat down

in front of the door.

"You can't get out,"

she said. "I will sit here

for another sixty years."

"I still like you!" shouted Mitchell

as he climbed out the window.

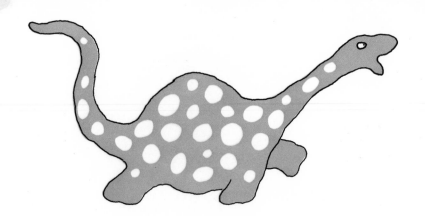

Margo called after him,
"I will glue you to your roof.
I will tie you
to your front door
with a thick green rope.
I will scotch-tape you,
paper-clip you to your house.
Then I will get
a gigantic rubber band
and loop you to your house.
I will not let you leave."

"I will unglue, untie, untape,
unclip and unloop myself,"
said Mitchell.
Mitchell ran around his house.
"I'm moving, moving, moving,"
he shouted.

Then he gathered up
some of the slimy moss near his house
and wrapped it in silver foil.
"Just in case there is no slimy moss
two weeks away."

Mitchell scooped up some mud
from a ditch.
"Maybe there is no mud
two weeks away.
Or no swamp water," he said
as he filled a plastic bag
with water from his swamp
and mud from his ditch.

Mitchell went into his house
and put the slimy moss
and mud and swamp water
into his suitcase.

The telephone rang.
Mitchell answered it.
"I will cement you
to your ceiling," said Margo,
and she hung up.

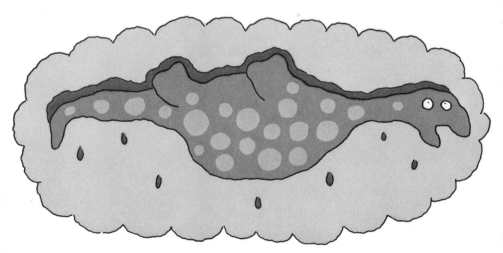

"I am beginning to think
that Margo does not want
me to move," said Mitchell
as he went back
to his packing.
He packed the
cap and mitten set
that Margo had given him.
"Maybe it will be cold
two weeks away," he thought.

Mitchell heard a shout.

He went to his window.

Margo was shouting,

"I will take you

to the laundromat

in my laundry bag,

and I will wash away

your idea of moving."

"Margo is a good shouter,"

thought Mitchell.

He remembered when
Margo had sent him
a Happy Birthday Shout
through the window:
"I'M GLAD YOU'RE THERE.
I'M GLAD I'M HERE.
HAPPY BIRTHDAY,
LOUD AND CLEAR."

"I wonder if there are any
Happy Birthday Shouters
two weeks away,"
thought Mitchell.

Mitchell held up the T-shirt
that Margo had given him.
It said,
MITCHELL, FRIEND OF MARGO
MARGO, FRIEND OF MITCHELL
"This shirt makes me feel sad
that I am moving," said Mitchell.
"But if I put it on
I won't have to look at it."
Mitchell put on the T-shirt.
"If I don't look down
at my chest,
I will feel all right."

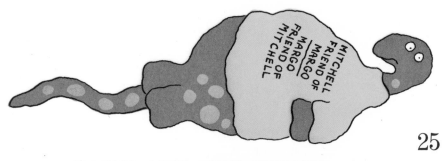

25

He closed his suitcase.

"There. I am all packed.

I am ready to go."

Mitchell walked through his house.

"So long, same old rooms," he said.

Mitchell took his suitcase

and went to Margo's house.

"I am all ready

to move," he said.

"I will stick you

to your house

with chewing gum,"

said Margo.

Mitchell picked up his suitcase

and ran.

"Good-by!" he called.

"I will write to you

every day."

Mitchell stopped running
and started to walk fast.
"I am a moving Mitchell,"
he said.
Mitchell walked and walked.

When night came,

he sent Margo a post card that said,

Dear Margo,

greetings from

one day away.

The second night he wrote,

Dear Margo,

more greetings from

two days away.

The third night he wrote,

    Dear Margo,

    more and more greetings

    from three days away.

"I am not much

    of a post-card writer,"

    thought Mitchell.

    But he sent more and more

    greetings to Margo

    each night.

At last Mitchell reached
two weeks away.
"I made it!" he said.

Mitchell built a house
and moved in.

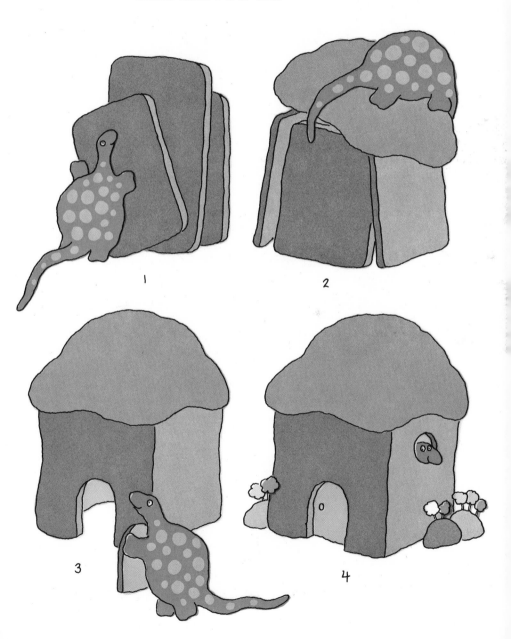

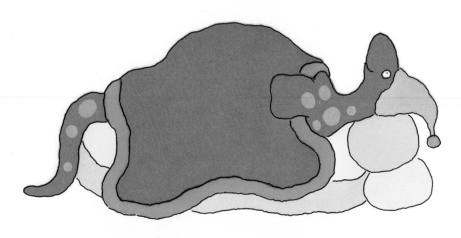

"I will go to bed right away
so I can wake up
in my new bedroom," he said.
"Mmm. New sleeps better,"
Mitchell said the next day.
"Now I will eat my first meal
in my new kitchen.
Mmm. New tastes better."

Mitchell went outside
and sat down in front of his house.
"This is a good house," he said.
"But there is something missing.
There is nobody next door.
What good is a good house
when there is nobody
next door to it?
I am lonely.
I miss Margo."

Mitchell wrote a post card to Margo:

Dear Margo,

the most greetings ever

from two weeks away.

The slimy moss is nice and slimy.

The mud is nice and thick.

The swamp water

is nice and mucky.

But I miss you.

Please come to see me.

Mitchell waited and waited.

And waited.

One morning he woke up

and saw a bottle of glue,

a thick green rope,

a big roll of Scotch tape,

a huge paper clip,

a gigantic rubber band,

a laundry bag,

a sack of cement

and a package of chewing gum.

Then he saw Margo.

"Mitchell!" said Margo.

"Margo!" said Mitchell.

"I am so happy to see you.

Here is my new house
and my new everything."
Mitchell showed Margo
his new house
and everything around it.

"Two weeks away is terrific,"
said Margo as she and Mitchell
ate breakfast.

"No, it isn't," said Mitchell.

"There is nobody next door."

"Oh," said Margo.

"I have the same problem
   where I am.
   There is nobody next door."

"I have an idea," said Mitchell,
and he got some twigs and mud.
"I have the same idea," said Margo,
and she filled her laundry bag
with more twigs and mud.

Then she got her bottle of glue,

thick green rope,

big roll of Scotch tape,

huge paper clip,

gigantic rubber band

and sack of cement.

"We can use these, too,"

she said.

Mitchell and Margo built a house
next door to Mitchell's house.

"Do you like it?" asked Mitchell.

"It's perfect," said Margo.

Margo moved into her new house.

She shouted,

"I'VE COME TO STAY

TWO WEEKS AWAY.

HAPPY BIRTHDAY."

It wasn't Mitchell's birthday.

But he was happy anyway.

MARJORIE WEINMAN SHARMAT's inimitable blend of humor and sensitivity has made her books popular with youngsters of all ages. Her other Ready-to-Read books include *Sophie and Gussie* and *The Trip*. For the picture-book age, she has written *I Don't Care*, and her older fans have enjoyed *A Visit With Rosalind* and *51 Sycamore Lane*, among many other books.

Ms. Sharmat lives in Arizona.

JOSE ARUEGO and ARIANE DEWEY have collaborated on an ever-growing list of beautiful picture books, including *The Chick and the Duckling, Mushroom in the Rain* and *Rum Pum Pum*. And they have illustrated *Sea Frog, City Frog*, among other books for beginning readers.

Both artists make their home in New York City.

Ready for fun?
Enjoy these Ready-to-Read animal tales.

WISH AGAIN, BIG BEAR
By Richard J. Margolis/Illustrated by Robert Lopshire
Clever Fish bargains with Big Bear for his life. "Readable and entertaining—good fare for even the slowest." —*School Library Journal*

THE KOMODO DRAGON'S JEWELS
Written and illustrated by Diane Redfield Massie
A great, green lizard causes an uproar aboard a cruise ship in "a rollicking tale of mistaken identity." —*School Library Journal*

THE STORY SNAIL
Written and illustrated by Anne Rockwell
"[This] interlocking chain-of-events story about a boy's quest for the silver snail that has taught him 100 stories....possesses an artless simplicity." —*Booklist*

SOPHIE AND GUSSIE
By Marjorie Weinman Sharmat/Illustrated by Lillian Hoban
Four funny episodes in the best friendship of two squirrels. "The illustrations are plentiful, the heroines lovable, and the effect enjoyable." —*Library Journal*

THE TRIP
And Other Sophie and Gussie Stories
By Marjorie Weinman Sharmat/Illustrated by Lillian Hoban
More comical stories about the scatter-brained, charming squirrels first met in *Sophie and Gussie.*

MITCHELL IS MOVING
By Marjorie Weinman Sharmat/Illustrated by Jose Aruego and Ariane Dewey
Mitchell the dinosaur finds that a new home is not all good if his neighbor Margo isn't there in a warm and funny story about friendship.

HARRY AND SHELLBURT
By Dorothy O. Van Woerkom/Illustrated by Erick Ingraham
A.L.A. Notable 1977. A hilarious re-running of the famous race between the tortoise and the hare. "A memorable beginning reader." —*Booklist* (starred review)

DONKEY YSABEL
By Dorothy O. Van Woerkom/Illustrated by Normand Chartier
Donkey Ysabel's pride is hurt when Papa brings home a car—but she manages to get the best of the "new donkey."

LITTLE NEW KANGAROO
By Bernard Wiseman/Illustrated by Robert Lopshire
With Mother Kangaroo lending a helpful pouch, a young kangaroo picks up four friends on his first jaunt into the Australian countryside.